Down the Rabbit Hole

from Alice's Adventures in Wonderland

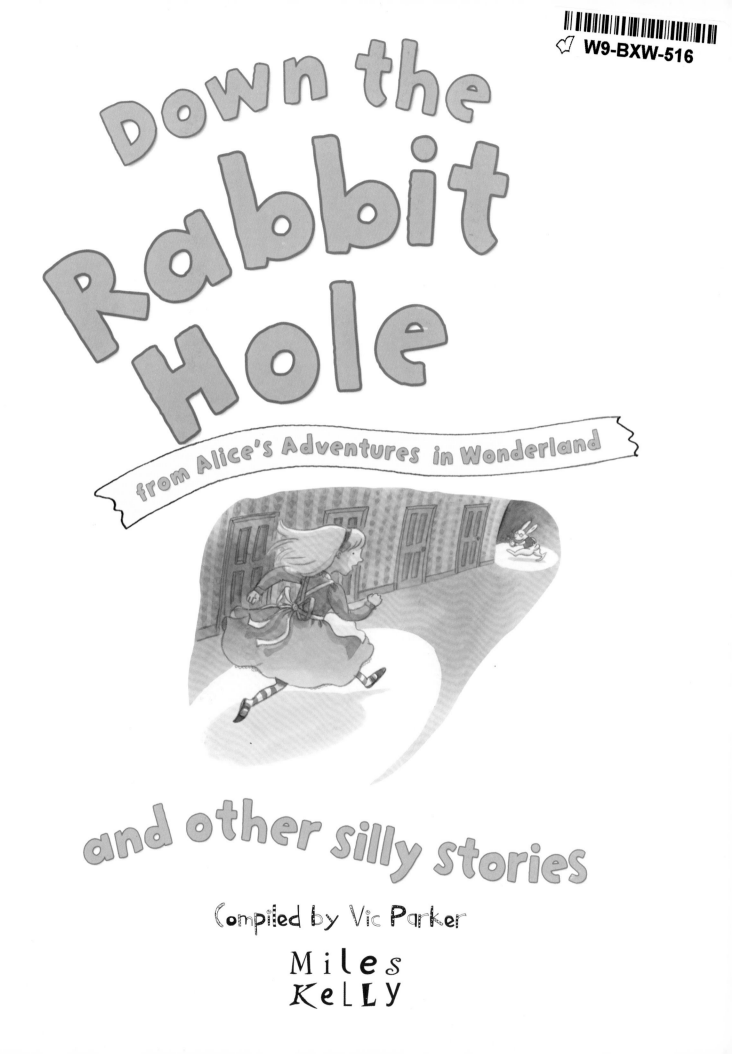

and other silly stories

Compiled by Vic Parker

Miles Kelly

First published in 2013 by Miles Kelly Publishing Ltd
Harding's Barn, Bardfield End Green, Thaxted, Essex, CM6 3PX, UK

2 4 6 8 10 9 7 5 3 1

Publishing Director Belinda Gallagher
Creative Director Jo Cowan
Editorial Director Rosie McGuire
Senior Editor Carly Blake
Editorial Assistant Amy Johnson
Designer Joe Jones
Production Manager Elizabeth Collins
Reprographics Stephan Davis, Jennifer Hunt, Thom Allaway

ISBN 978-1-84810-924-7

Printed in China

British Library Cataloguing-in-Publication Data
A catalogue record for this book is available from the British Library

ACKNOWLEDGMENTS

The publishers would like to thank the following artists who have contributed to this book:

Beehive Illustration Agency: Rosie Brooks, Mike Phillips
The Bright Agency: Michael Garton
Jan Lewis (inc. cover), Aimee Mappley (decorative frames)

All other artwork from the Miles Kelly Artwork Bank

Made with paper from a sustainable forest

www.mileskelly.net   info@mileskelly.net

www.factsforprojects.com

Contents

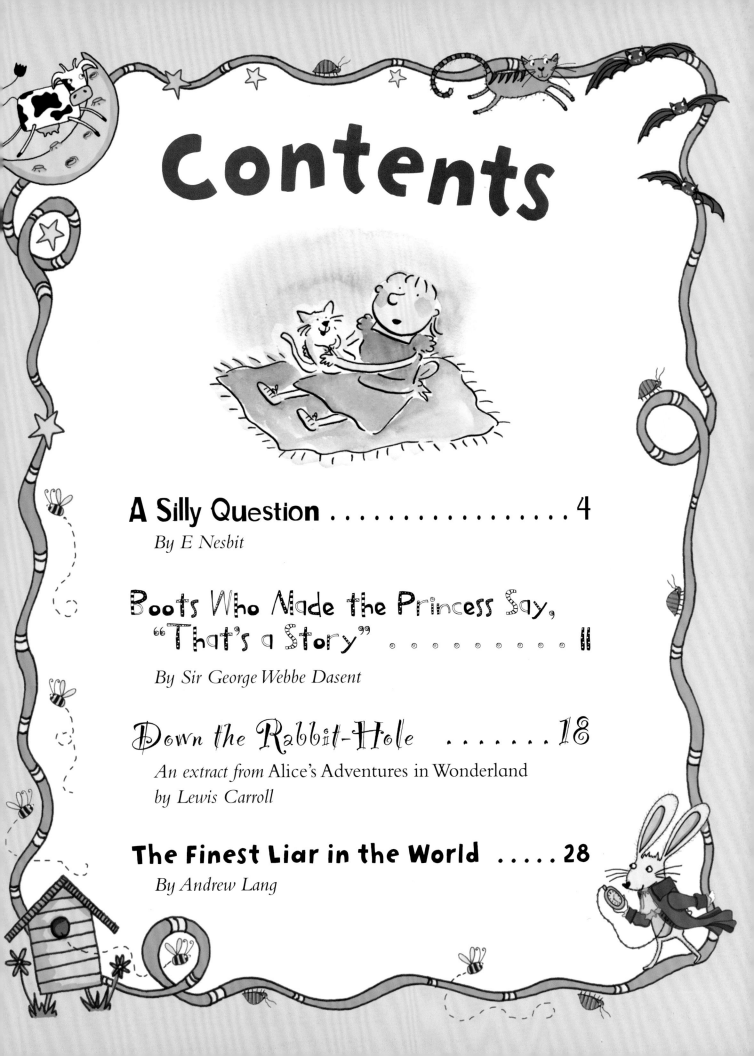

A Silly Question

By E Nesbit

"How do you come to be white, when all your brothers are tabby?" Dolly asked her kitten. As she spoke, she took it away from the ball it was playing with, and held it up and looked in its face as Alice did with the Red Queen.

"I'll tell you if you'll keep it a secret, and not hold me so tight," the kitten answered. Dolly was not surprised to hear the kitten speak, for she had read fairy books and she knew that all creatures answer if one only speaks to them properly. So she held the kitten more comfortably and the tale began.

"You must know, my dear Dolly," the kitten began, sounding as though it had always known Dolly very well, "you must know that when we were very small we all set out to seek our fortunes—"

"Why," interrupted Dolly, "you were all born and brought up in our barn! I used to see you every day."

"Quite so," said the kitten, "we sought our fortune every night, and it turned out to be mice, mostly. Well, one night I was seeking mine, when I came to a hole in the door that I had never noticed before. I crept through it and found myself in a beautiful large room. It smelled delicious. There was cheese there, and fish, and cream, and mice, and milk. It was the most lovely room you can think of."

"There's no such room—" began Dolly.

"Well, I stayed there some time," continued the kitten. "It was the happiest hour of my life. But, as I was washing my face after one of the most delicious herring's heads you ever tasted, I noticed that on nails all round the room were hung skins – and they were cat skins," the kitten added slowly. "Well may you tremble!"

Dolly hadn't trembled. She had only shaken the kitten to make it speak faster.

"Well, I stood there rooted to the ground with horror, and then came a sort of horrible scramble-rush, and a barking and squeaking, and a terrible monster stood before me. It was something like a dog and something like a broom, something like being thrown out of the larder by cook – I can't describe it. It caught me up, and in less

7

than a moment it had hung my tabby skin on a nail behind the door. I crept out of that lovely fairyland a cat without a skin. And that's how I came to be white."

"I don't quite see—" began Dolly.

"No? Why, what would your mother do if someone took off your dress, and hung it on a nail where she could not get it?"

"Buy me another, I suppose."

"Exactly. But when my mother took me to the cat-skin shop, they were, unfortunately, quite out of tabby dresses in my size, so I had to have a white one."

"I don't believe a word of it," said Dolly.

"No? Well, I'm sure it's as good a story as you could expect in answer to such a silly question."

"But you were always—"

"Oh, well!" said the kitten, showing its claws, "if you know more about it than I do, of course there's no more to be said. Perhaps you could tell me why your hair is brown?"

"I was born so, I believe," said Dolly gently.

The kitten put its nose in the air.

"You've got no imagination," it said.

"But Kitty, really and truly, without pretending, you were born white, you know."

"If you know all about it, why did you ask me? At any rate, you can't expect me to remember whether I was born white or not. I was too young to notice such things."

"Now you are in fun," said poor Dolly, bewildered.

The kitten bristled with indignation.

"What! You really don't believe me? I'll never speak to you again," the kitten said. And it never has.

Boots Who Made the Princess Say, "That's a Story"

By Sir George Webbe Dasent

Once on a time there was a king who had a daughter, and she was such a dreadful storyteller that the like of her was not to be found far or near. So the king sent out word that if anyone could tell such a string of lies that would get her to say, "That's a story," he could have her for his wife, and half the kingdom too. Many came to try their luck, for everyone would have been very glad to have the Princess, to say nothing of the kingdom. But they all cut a sorry figure, for the Princess was so given to storytelling that their lies went in one ear and out the other.

Among the rest came three brothers. The two elder went first, but they fared no better than those who had gone before. Last of all, the third brother, Boots, set off and found the Princess in the farmyard.

"Good morning," he said, "and thank you for nothing."

"Good morning," said she, "and the same to you."

Then she went on, "You haven't such a fine farmyard as ours, I'll be bound. For when two shepherds stand, one at each end of it, and blow their ram's horns, one can't hear the other."

"Haven't we though!" answered Boots. "Ours is far bigger. For when a cow begins to go with calf at one end of it, she doesn't get to the other end before the time to drop her calf is come."

"I dare say!" said the Princess. "Well, but you haven't such a big ox, after all, as ours yonder. For when two men sit, one on each horn, they can't touch each other with a ginormous ruler."

"Stuff!" said Boots. "Is that all? Why, we have an ox who is so big, that when two men sit, one on each horn, and each blows his great mountain trumpet, they can't hear one another."

"I dare say," said the Princess. "But you haven't so much milk as we, I'll be bound.

14

For we milk our cattle into great pails, and carry them indoors and empty them into great tubs, and so we make great, great cheeses."

"Oh! you do, do you?" said Boots. "Well, we milk ours into great tubs, and then we put them in carts and drive them indoors, and then we turn them out into great brewing vats, and so we make cheeses as

big as a great house. We had, too, a pony to
tread the cheese well together when it was
making, but once she tumbled down into
the cheese, and we lost her. After we had
eaten at this cheese seven years, we came
upon the pony, alive and kicking.

"Well, once after that I was going to
drive this pony to the mill, and her
backbone snapped in two, but I wasn't put
out, not I, for I took a young tree, and put it
into her for a backbone, and she had no
other backbone all the while we had her.
But the sapling grew up into such a tall
tree, that I climbed right up to heaven by it,
and when I got there, I saw the Virgin Mary
sitting and spinning the foam of the sea into
pigs'-bristle ropes. But just then the tree

broke short off, and I couldn't get down again, so the Virgin Mary let me down by one of the ropes. Down I slipped, straight into a fox's hole, and who should sit there but my mother and your father cobbling shoes. Just as I stepped in, my mother gave your father such a box on the ear, that it made his whiskers curl."

"That's a story!" said the Princess. "My father never did any such thing in all his born days!"

So Boots got to marry the Princess and won half the kingdom besides.

Down the Rabbit-Hole

An extract from *Alice's Adventures in Wonderland*
by Lewis Carroll

Alice was beginning to get very tired of sitting by her sister on the bank, and of having nothing to do. Once or twice she had peeped into the book her sister was reading, but it had no pictures or conversations in it. 'And what is the use of a book,' thought Alice, 'without pictures or conversation?'

So she was considering (as well as she

could, for the hot day made her feel very sleepy and stupid) whether the pleasure of making a daisy-chain would be worth the trouble of getting up and picking the daisies, when suddenly a White Rabbit with pink eyes ran close by her.

There was nothing so *very* remarkable in that. Nor did Alice think it so *very* much out of the way to hear the Rabbit say to itself, "Oh dear! Oh dear! I shall be late!" (When she thought it over afterward, it occurred to her that she ought to have wondered at this, but at the time it all seemed quite natural.) When the Rabbit actually *took a watch out of its waistcoat-pocket*, looked at it, and then hurried on, Alice started to her feet, for it flashed across her mind that she had never seen a rabbit with either a waistcoat-pocket or a watch to take out of it. Burning with curiosity, she ran across the field after it, and fortunately was just in time to see it pop down a large rabbit-hole under the hedge.

In another moment down went Alice after it. The rabbit-hole went straight on like a tunnel for some way, and then dipped suddenly down, so that Alice had not a moment to think about stopping herself before she found herself falling down a well.

First, she tried to look down and make out what she was coming to, but it was too dark to see anything. Then she looked at the sides of the well, and noticed that they were filled with cupboards and bookshelves. Here and there she saw maps and pictures

hung upon pegs. She took down a jar from one of the shelves as she passed. It was labelled ORANGE MARMALADE, but to her great disappointment it was empty. She did not like to drop the jar for fear of killing somebody, so managed to put it into one of the cupboards as she fell past it.

'Well!' thought Alice to herself. 'After such a fall as this, I shall think nothing of tumbling down stairs! How brave they'll all think me at home! Why, I wouldn't say anything about it, even if I fell off the top of the house!' (Which was very likely true.)

Down, down, down. Would the fall *never* come to an end? "I wonder how many miles I've fallen by this time?" she said aloud. "I must be getting somewhere near the center of the earth. Let me see, that would be four thousand miles down, I think…" (For, you see, Alice had learned several things of this sort in her lessons in the schoolroom, and though this was not a *very* good opportunity for showing off her knowledge, as there was no one to listen to her, still it was good practice to say it over.) "Yes, that's about the right distance – but then I wonder what latitude or longitude I've got to?" (Alice had no idea what latitude was, or longitude either, but thought they were nice grand words to say.)

Presently she began again. "I wonder if I shall fall right *through* the earth! How funny it'll seem to come out among the people that walk with their heads downward! But I shall have to ask them what the name of the country is, you know. Please, Ma'am, is this New Zealand or Australia?" (And she tried to curtsey as she spoke – fancy *curtseying* as you're falling through the air! Do you think you could manage it?) "And what an ignorant little girl she'll think me for asking! No, it'll never do to ask, but perhaps I shall see it written up somewhere."

Down, down, down. There was nothing else to do, so Alice soon began talking again. "Dinah'll miss me very much tonight, I should think!" (Dinah was the cat.) "I hope they'll remember her saucer of milk at tea-time. Dinah my dear! I wish you were down here with me! There are no mice in the air, I'm afraid, but you might catch a bat, and that's very like a mouse, you know. But do cats eat bats, I wonder?"

Alice began to get rather sleepy, and went on saying to herself, in a dreamy sort of way, "Do cats eat bats?" and sometimes, "Do bats eat cats?" (For, you see, as she couldn't answer either question, it didn't much matter which way she put it.)

She felt that she was dozing off, and had just begun to dream that she was walking hand in hand with Dinah, and saying to her very earnestly, "Now, Dinah, tell me the truth: did you ever eat a bat?" when suddenly, *thump! thump!* Down she came upon a heap of sticks and dry leaves, and the fall was over.

Alice was not a bit hurt, and she jumped up on to her feet in a moment. She looked up, but it was all dark overhead. Before her was another long passage, and the White Rabbit was still in sight, hurrying down it. There was not a moment to be lost: away went Alice like the wind, and was just in time to hear it say, as it turned a corner, "Oh my ears and whiskers, how late it's getting!"

She was close behind it when she turned the corner, but the

Rabbit was no longer to be seen. She found herself in a long, low hall, which was lit up by a row of lamps hanging from the roof.

There were doors all round the hall, but they were all locked, and when Alice had been all the way down one side and up the other, trying every door, she walked sadly down the middle, wondering how she was ever to get out again…

27

The Finest Liar in the World

By Andrew Lang

At the edge of a wood there lived an old man who had only one son. One day he called the boy to him and said he wanted some corn ground, but the youth must be sure never to enter any mill where the miller was beardless.

The boy took the corn and set out.

Before he had gone very far he saw a large mill in front of him, with a beardless man standing in the doorway.

"Good greeting, beardless one!" cried he.

"Good greeting, sonny," replied the man.

"Could I grind something here?"

"Yes, certainly! I will finish what I am doing and then you can grind as long as you like."

But suddenly the boy remembered what his father had told him, and bade farewell to the man. He went further down the river till he came to another mill,

29

not knowing that as soon as his back was turned the beardless man had picked up a bag of corn and run hastily to the same mill before him.

When the boy reached the second mill, and saw a second beardless man sitting there, he did not stop, and walked on till he came to a third mill. But this time also the beardless man had been too clever for him, and had arrived first by another road. When it happened a fourth time the boy grew cross. He said to himself, "It is no good going on. There seems to be a beardless man in every mill," and he took his sack from his back, and made up his mind to grind his corn where he was.

The beardless man finished grinding his

own corn, and when he had done he said to the boy, who was beginning to grind his, "Suppose, sonny, we make a cake of what you have there."

Now the boy had been rather uneasy when he remembered his father's words, but he thought to himself, 'What is done cannot be undone,' and answered, "Very well, let it be."

Then the beardless one got up, threw the flour into the tub and made a hole in the middle, telling the boy to fetch some water from the river in his two hands to mix the cake. When the cake was ready for baking they put it on the fire, and covered it with hot ashes, till it was cooked through. Then they leaned it up against the wall, for it was too big to go into a cupboard, and the beardless one said to the boy: "Look here, sonny, if we share this cake we shall neither of us have enough. Let us see who can tell the biggest lie, and the one who lies the best shall have the whole cake."

The boy, not knowing what else to do, answered, "All right, you begin."

So the beardless one began to lie with all his might, and when he was tired of inventing new lies the boy said to him, "My good fellow, if *that* is all you can do it is not much! Listen to me, and I will tell you a true story.

"In my youth, when I was an old man, we had a quantity of beehives. Every morning when I got up I counted them over, and it was quite easy to number the bees, but I never could reckon the hives properly. One day, as I was counting the bees, I discovered that my best bee was missing, and without losing a moment I saddled a rooster and went out to look for him. I traced him as far as the shore, and knew that he had crossed the sea, and that I must follow. When I had reached the other side I found a man had harnessed my bee to a plow, and with his help was sowing millet seed.

"I shouted to him, 'That is my bee! Where did you get him from?'

"The man replied, 'Brother, if he is yours, take him,' and he not only gave me back my bee, but a sack of millet seed into the bargain, because he had made use of my bee. Then I put the bag on my shoulders, took the saddle from the rooster and placed it on the back of the bee, which I mounted, leading the rooster by a string, so that he should have a rest. As we were flying home over the sea one of the strings that held the bag of millet broke in two, and the sack dropped straight into the ocean. It was quite lost, of course, and there was no use thinking about it, and by the time we were safe back again night had come. I then got down from my bee, and let him loose so that he might get his supper, gave the rooster some hay, and went to sleep myself. But when I awoke with the sun what a scene met my eyes! During the night, wolves had come and had eaten my bee. And honey lay ankle-deep in the valley and knee-deep on the hills. Then I began to consider how I could best collect some to take home with me.

"Now it happened that I had with me a small hatchet, and this I took to the wood, hoping to meet some animal which I could kill, whose skin I might turn into a bag. As I entered the forest I saw two roe deer hopping on one foot, so I slew them with a single blow, and made three bags from their skins, all of which I filled with honey and placed on the back of the rooster.

"At length I reached home, where I was told that my father had just been born, and that I must go to fetch some holy water to sprinkle him with. As I went I turned over in my mind if there was no way for me to get back my millet seed, which had dropped into the sea. When I arrived at the place with the holy water I saw the seed had fallen on fruitful soil, and was growing before my eyes. More than that, it was cut by an invisible hand and made into a cake.

"So I took the cake as well as the holy water, and was flying back with them over the sea, when there fell a great rain, and the sea was swollen, and swept away my millet cake. Ah, how annoyed I was at its loss when I was safe on earth again.

"Suddenly I remembered that my hair was very long. If I stood it touched the ground, although if I was sitting it only reached my ears. I seized a knife and cut off a large lock, which I plaited together, and, when night came, tied it into a knot and prepared to use it for a pillow. But what was I to do for a fire? A tinder box I had, but no wood. Then it occurred to me that I had stuck a needle in my clothes, so I took the needle and split it in pieces, and lit it, then laid myself down by the fire and went to sleep. But while I was sleeping a spark from the fire lighted on the hair, which was burned up in a moment. In despair I threw myself on the ground, and instantly sank in it as far as my waist. I struggled to get out but only fell in further, so I ran to the house, seized a spade, dug myself out, and took home the holy water.

"On the way I noticed that the ripe fields were full of reapers, and suddenly the air became so frightfully hot that the men dropped down in a faint. Then I called to them, 'Why don't you bring out our mare, which is as tall as two days and as broad as half a day, and make a shade for yourselves?' My father heard what I said and jumped quickly on the mare, and the reapers worked with a will in the shadow, while I snatched up a wooden pail to bring them some water to drink.

"When I got to the well it was frozen hard. In order to draw some water I had to take off my head and break the ice with it. As I drew near them, carrying the water, the reapers all cried out, 'What has become of your head?' I put up my hand and discovered that I really had no head, and that I must have left it in the well. I ran back for it, but found that a fox which was passing by had pulled my head out of the water and was tearing at it. I crept up to him, and gave him such a kick that he uttered a loud scream, and let fall a parchment on which was written: THE CAKE IS MINE AND THE BEARDLESS ONE GOES EMPTY-HANDED."

With these words the boy rose, took the cake, and went home, while the beardless one was left to swallow his disappointment.